Simon
Ellis,
Spelling Bee
Champ

Franklin School Friends

Simon Ellis, Spelling Bee Champ

Claudia Mills

pictures by Rob Shepperson

SQUARE
FISH

Margaret Ferguson Books

Farrar Straus Giroux • New York

Special thanks to Lisa Graff and Susan Dobinick
for their help with the honey pie recipe.

SQUARE FISH

An Imprint of Macmillan
175 Fifth Avenue
New York, NY 10010
mackids.com

Our books may be purchased in bulk for promotional, educational, or
business use. Please contact your local bookseller or the Macmillan
Corporate and Premium Sales Department at (800) 221-7945 ext. 5442
or by e-mail at MacmillanSpecialMarkets@macmillan.com.

Library of Congress Cataloging-in-Publication Data

Mills, Claudia.
    Simon Ellis, spelling bee champ / Claudia Mills ; pictures by
Rob Shepperson.
        pages cm. — (Franklin School friends ; 4)
    Summary: Simon Ellis and the rest of the third grade Franklin
School Friends participate in a spelling bee where Simon's
competitive spirit takes over until he realizes that sometimes the
best way to win is to take a chance and let other people shine.
    ISBN 978-1-250-08858-1 (paperback)
    ISBN 978-0-374-30222-1 (ebook)
    [1. Spelling bees—Fiction.   2. Competition (Psychology)—
Fiction.   3. Winning and losing—Fiction.]   I. Shepperson, Rob,
illustrator.   II. Title.

PZ7.M63963Sp 2015
[Fic]—dc23

2015002961

Originally published in the United States by Farrar Straus Giroux
First Square Fish Edition: 2016
Book designed by Elizabeth H. Clark
Square Fish logo designed by Filomena Tuosto

1   3   5   7   9   10   8   6   4   2

For Gregory, who invented Bird War

Simon Ellis, Spelling Bee Champ

1

Simon Ellis sat sprawled on the floor next to Jackson Myers, trying to make his best friend in the whole world plunge to his doom.

It was Sunday afternoon, and they were at Jackson's house, video game controllers in hand, playing Jackson's newest game, Galaxy Warriors. Simon was warrior Xalik, and Jackson was warrior Satu. If either player was knocked off his platform in interstellar space, it would mean instant death.

Xalik fired his laser beam at Satu.

Satu ducked.

Satu shot a string of fireballs at Xalik.

Xalik sprang over the top of them and countered with another quick laser.

Zing!

Satu flew backward and fell, then leaped up again to fire another torrent of fireballs at Xalik.

"Wait!" Jackson paused the game to dart after his ferret, Ferrari, who was scrambling out the door of his bedroom and heading toward the stairs. Simon waited to save Xalik from defeat, disgrace, and death as Jackson headed after his pet.

Simon and Jackson had been best friends since preschool. They usually played at Jackson's house, because Jackson was the only one who had a game system, plus a big TV in his room to play it on. What Simon's room had instead of a TV was two tall bookcases crammed full of books, most of which Simon had read. Simon wondered what it would be like to have two tall bookcases *and* a big TV. There was no rule saying that if you had one, you couldn't have the other.

Jackson returned with Ferrari, careful to shut his bedroom door this time. The little ferret scrabbled down Jackson's arm and up Simon's. Simon used to be nervous around Ferrari, but he had worked hard to get comfortable with having a small furry creature climbing all over him. Now Ferrari was his second-best friend after Jackson.

Simon thought he had a good chance of beating Jackson at Galaxy Warriors today. Jackson played video games more often than Simon did, but Galaxy Warriors was a brand-new game, so the two boys were evenly matched.

Besides, Simon was coordinated with his hands from playing the violin for four years, starting at age five. Plus, he was just good at strategy. Once he started playing a game, even if Jackson had a head start, he caught on quickly. Just the way he caught on quickly to fractions and decimals in math, or could memorize all fifty states and their state capitals, or get a perfect score on practically every spelling test.

"Ready?" Jackson asked, picking up his controller again.

"Ready!" Simon replied.

Xalik fell back, landing inches away from the edge of the platform.

No!

Then Xalik recovered from his fall and ducked more of Satu's fireballs.

He unleashed one last powerful laser beam at Satu.

Satu flew far off the end of the platform and plunged into space.

Victory for Xalik!

Simon felt himself beaming. He scooped up

Ferrari and wiggled him in the air like a victory trophy.

"Do you want to be Xalik next time, and I'll be Satu?" he asked.

Jackson didn't answer.

When Simon turned to look at him, Jackson was scowling.

"What?" Simon asked. Was he holding Ferrari the wrong way? Gently, he set Ferrari down on the carpet beside Jackson.

But Jackson's scowl only deepened. "If you're Xalik, Xalik wins. If you're Satu, Satu wins. Doesn't it ever get boring, winning all the time?"

Simon didn't know what to say.

"Because it sure gets boring losing all the time," Jackson muttered.

Simon found his voice as the little ferret climbed up Jackson's leg. "I don't win all the time. Nobody wins all the time."

"Name one time you've ever lost at anything."

Simon couldn't believe Jackson had to ask this. "I lost at Amphibian Apocalypse last week. Remember? You beat me three times in a row."

"Because you had never played the game *ever*, and I'd played it like ten thousand times, and then after I beat you three times, you beat me *four* times in a row."

"But you still beat me three times first," Simon reminded him.

Jackson picked up Ferrari and dropped him back in the wire cage that stood on a low table next to the bed. He shut the cage door with an angry click, as if it were poor Ferrari's fault that Simon/Xalik had fired his laser so well. Jackson was being unfair not only to Simon but to Ferrari, too.

"You said to name one time I didn't win, and I just named three," Simon said, hoping that

Jackson would stop being mad. But even though this was completely true, Jackson's expression didn't change.

"You don't even have a game system in your house," Jackson said, his tone accusing.

That was true, too, but it meant that *Simon* was the one who had something to complain about. Jackson was the luckier kid, with a TV, a game system, *and* a ferret of his own.

"And you still beat me at video games!" Jackson said. "You're better than I am at math. And reading. And spelling. Oh, and running."

Simon couldn't deny it. But he just happened to love math, reading, spelling, and running. It made sense that if you loved something, you'd keep on doing it, and then you'd get good at it. He tried to think of something Jackson was better at.

"You're better than I am at soccer," he offered. Jackson's soccer team had made the playoffs this spring.

"You don't play soccer!" Jackson retorted.

"So I'm not better at it!"

"But if you *did* play soccer, you *would* be," Jackson said wearily.

Jackson turned off the TV and made a big show of setting the game controllers side by side on the bureau, even though he usually left them on the floor for his little brother to trip over.

What was Simon supposed to say?

Okay, maybe he didn't lose at very many things. But he did lose sometimes.

And right now he was afraid he might be starting to lose his best friend.

On Monday morning, Simon was glad to see Jackson waiting for him as usual on the blacktop outside Franklin School before the first bell, even though Jackson had still been cross when Mrs. Ellis had come to pick Simon up right after their quarrel.

"Hey," Jackson said, giving Simon a sheepish smile.

"Hey," Simon said, with a sheepish smile of his own.

Maybe things were going to be okay with Jackson, after all.

After the flag salute and morning announcements, their third-grade teacher, Mrs. Molina, told the class to listen closely to the news she was about to share. Mrs. Molina was strict. She even looked strict, with wire-framed glasses and hair pulled back sternly from her face. But Simon liked her.

"Class, a week from this Friday is our Franklin School spelling bee. You'll be competing against the other third-grade classes."

Simon felt a jolt of excitement. He had never been in a spelling bee before. The Franklin School bee was just for third, fourth, and fifth graders.

"What do we get if we win?" one kid asked.

"The *main* thing you'll get will be the satisfaction of being such good spellers."

Simon's classmates looked disappointed.

"But Mr. Boone has also come up with a special prize that he'll tell you about later."

Now the class cheered. They all loved their chubby, funny, always-enthusiastic principal.

"Is everyone going to spell in the bee?" Kelsey Green asked. "Or do our best spellers compete against the best spellers in the other classes?"

Simon knew that Kelsey loved reading and spelling as much as he did.

"Each class will be divided into teams, and everyone competes, working together as team members."

Simon didn't like the sound of that. He never signed up for team sports like soccer or basketball. He preferred individual sports like running, where how you did was totally up to you alone.

"But our strongest spellers will certainly have an important role to play," Mrs. Molina added.

"Si-mon! Si-mon!" someone started to chant.

Kelsey tossed her short brown hair. Simon knew she wanted the chant to be "Kel-sey! Kel-sey!" But he couldn't help flushing with pride at hearing his classmates treat him as their star speller.

Then he heard Cody Harmon mutter, "Super Simon. Super-Duper-Pooper Simon." Cody was the worst in the class at most of the things Simon was best at.

Simon thought he heard Jackson laugh. But maybe it was somebody else.

Simon pretended he hadn't heard, but Cody's comment stung, and Jackson's laugh, if it had been Jackson who laughed, stung even more.

2

Mr. Boone popped his head into Mrs. Molina's room after lunch. Actually, he popped his whole self into the room. Some of Simon's favorite words to describe Mr. Boone were *exuberant*, *ebullient*, and *effervescent* (though he wasn't quite sure if *ebullient* had one *l* or two, and if *effervescent* had one *f* or two). Was there a reason that so many words that meant *energetic* and *exciting* started with the letter *e*?

"Boys and girls!" Mr. Boone boomed. "It's t-i-m-e for the annual Franklin S-c-h-o-o-l spelling b-e-e!"

The class laughed, not so much because that was a funny thing to say, but because it was funny Mr. Boone who said it.

"Who's a good speller here?"

Hands flew up, although Simon knew for a fact that half the class was terrible at spelling. Jackson sometimes wrote *there* for *their* or *they're*. Cody mixed up *to*, *two*, and *too*, practically the shortest words in the entire dictionary. The only words shorter than *to* were *a* and *I*, which even Cody didn't misspell.

Cody, Simon noticed, was the only kid in the class who hadn't raised his hand in response to Mr. Boone's question. At least Cody was honest.

"Who likes pie?" Mr. Boone asked then.

This time every single hand went up, including Cody's.

"Well," Mr. Boone said, "I myself am a terrible speller."

Simon doubted that was true. How could

someone who wasn't good at spelling get picked to be a principal? You'd think a principal would have to be good at every subject taught in school. Maybe someday he himself would be a principal.

"But," Mr. Boone went on, "I am very good at baking pies. Too good, in fact."

He patted his round middle regretfully as the class laughed again.

"So," Mr. Boone said, "I'm going to invite the winning team in each grade to be my guests at a pie buffet featuring pies baked by yours truly." He pointed to himself.

"What about the teams that don't win?" Jackson asked. "They'll want pie, too."

Mr. Boone thought for a moment. As a pie lover, he seemed to think it quite reasonable that everybody would want to eat pie.

"All right," he finally said. "If I see everybody trying his or her b-e-s-t, busily studying all your spelling w-o-r-d-s, I might be able to come up with a piece of pie for everyone. But only the members of the winning team will get the full pie buffet with my famous *honey* pie. Or else it wouldn't be a prize for a spelling *bee*, right? Does that sound fair? Now, I know Mrs. Molina has a lot of m-a-t-h she wants to t-e-a-c-h you."

Mrs. Molina always had a lot of math she wanted to teach.

"So I'll b-u-z-z on over to another c-l-a-s-s."

And then Mr. Boone was gone, buzzing loudly as he departed.

Simon had never tasted honey pie, but it certainly sounded like the best possible prize for success in a spelling bee.

He raised his hand, and Mrs. Molina called on him.

"How are you going to pick the teams?" he asked.

Mrs. Molina adjusted her glasses. Simon recognized that as her favorite stalling technique.

"The other teachers and I are still figuring that out. We're meeting after school today to finalize the plans."

Why did there have to be teams at all? Why not just let the best spellers stand up in front of everybody and spell, the way Simon had seen kids do in the televised finals of the National Spelling Bee?

He thought about raising his hand to ask Mrs. Molina if there *had* to be teams. If the teachers hadn't figured out how to set up the teams, maybe there was still time to change their minds so that kids could compete as individuals. That way he and Kelsey could go word-to-word against each other, nice and simple. The best speller would win. Maybe it would be Kelsey. Maybe it would be Simon. Either way,

Simon's success or failure wouldn't have to depend on anyone else.

But he didn't want Cody to make another crack about "Super Simon" and hear Jackson laugh.

Instead, he listened as Mrs. Molina told the class that she was going to clear off the big bulletin board at the back of the room to make a word wall. It would be covered with blank paper on which everybody could write his or her favorite words, starting on Wednesday.

"We want to make the next couple of weeks a big, wonderful word party," Mrs. Molina finished, sounding almost as enthusiastic as Mr. Boone himself. "Don't post our regular third-grade spelling words on the word wall. Go on a word hunt for the best, juiciest words you can find."

"Can we write as many words as we want?" Simon asked.

Maybe that was a Super Simon question, too. But he couldn't help himself.

Mrs. Molina smiled. "The more words, the merrier! During the bee, we'll start with some of the spelling words you've been tested on all year. But then, if no teams are getting eliminated because those words are too easy, we'll move on to more challenging words taken from the word walls in the three third-grade classrooms. So do your best to find words that can stump the other teams."

As Mrs. Molina turned to the math lesson, Simon jotted down some amazing words that he could write on the class word wall.

He started with all those great *e* words for describing Mr. Boone. Then he added even more excellent *e* words to the list:

Exhilarating. He hoped he had spelled that one right. Did it have an *e* in the middle, after the *l*, or was the *a* correct?

Elating.

Electrifying.

All words Simon would use to describe a spelling bee, even if it had to have teams.

After school Simon had his violin lesson.

Jackson didn't take private music lessons, though he had told Simon that he wanted to play the tuba when they started instrumental music in fourth grade. Simon could imagine his friend blowing into the huge brass tuba, puffing out his cheeks as fat as he could. Just the thought of it made him chuckle.

Simon's violin teacher, Dr. Lee, was from Korea. She wasn't a medical doctor. She was a doctor of playing the violin.

"So what is new with you this week, Mr. Simon Ellis?" she asked as he hung up his jacket on the hook by the entrance to her studio.

Simon told her about the spelling bee.

"Ah," she said. "We can spell words in the language of music, too, you know."

She picked up her violin and played four notes. Each note was a beautiful, shimmering thing when Dr. Lee played it.

"Did you recognize the word?" she asked.

Simon didn't.

She played the first note again.

"F," she said.

The next note was higher.

"A."

The note after that was lower.

"C."

The final note was higher than the note she had just played but lower than the note she played first.

"E?" Simon guessed. *"Face!"*

He liked the idea of spelling words this way. Of course, the only letters of the musical

alphabet were the notes of the scale: C, D, E, F, G, A, B. Still, there were a lot of words you could spell with those letters. *Bed. Bead. Feed. Beg. Cab. Gab. Bee.*

It would be so cool to be able to send a message to a friend in the secret code of music. Maybe once Jackson started playing the tuba, Jackson's tuba and Simon's violin could talk together in their own private language and puzzle everyone else.

But Simon didn't know if Jackson would think that idea was as cool as he did, or if he would think it was dumb.

As he took his violin out of its case, Simon remembered back to second grade when he and Jackson had their own private game called Bird War. It was a game they invented themselves, played in the backseat of the car while one of their parents was driving them somewhere.

Each boy took a stuffed toy bird and placed

it on top of the seat in front. When the driver at the wheel turned around a corner, one of the birds, or both, might fall off its perch. If Simon's bird fell off and Jackson's bird didn't, Jackson got a point. If Jackson's bird fell off and Simon's bird didn't, Simon got a point.

Back when they played Bird War all the time, Simon's bird fell tons of times, every bit as often as Jackson's bird did. But they hadn't played Bird War in a while. Simon was afraid that if he mentioned it, Jackson would say, "Bird War is stupid."

Just as Jackson might say that a secret language for a tuba and a violin was stupid.

"Simon?" Dr. Lee asked, interrupting his thoughts.

Simon picked up his bow and began to play his scale for the week, trying to make each note sound as pure and glowing as Dr. Lee's notes had been.

3

At school the next day Simon beamed a secret, silent message of his own to Mrs. Molina: *No teams! No teams!*

Even as he did it, he knew it was a silly thing to do. The teachers had already met after school yesterday to decide whatever they were going to decide. It was too late to change their minds now.

Sure enough, Mrs. Molina told the class, "Each of you will compete in the spelling bee on a team with four members."

Oh, well.

Then Simon cheered up. Maybe he and Kelsey could be on the same team, with two of the other best spellers in the class. Maybe the four best spellers in the class could all be on a team together!

But if he and Jackson were on different teams and Simon's team won, Jackson would be *really* mad at him, even madder than he had been when Simon beat him at Galaxy Warriors. At least the Galaxy Warriors winner didn't get the reward of Mr. Boone's pie buffet.

Mrs. Molina picked up a piece of paper and said, "Here are your teams."

Simon listened, tense, as she began to read.

"Kelsey Green, Izzy Barr"—the two girls beamed—"Ryan Alito, and Tyler Tedesco."

Simon tried to figure out the teacher's reasoning. She had put some friends together (Kelsey and her best friend Izzy), but not all friends (not Kelsey's other best friend, Annika). There was a mix of girls and boys, a mix of good spellers (Kelsey and Ryan) and not-so-good spellers (Izzy and Tyler).

He felt sorry for whichever team got stuck with Cody.

His ears strained to hear his own name as Mrs. Molina read out the next team, and the team after that.

Then: "Simon Ellis, Jackson Myers . . ." He was relieved that Jackson flashed him a big grin. "Annika Riz . . ." Annika was great at math, as good as Simon, but not as great at spelling. "And Cody Harmon."

Terrible! The absolute worst!

If Simon's team went down in flames over *to*, *two*, and *too*, he couldn't bear it. But he was so grateful to be on the same team with Jackson that relief swamped disappointment.

Simon waited until the last team had been

announced, and then he raised his hand. "So how do the teams actually work?" he asked.

"Good question," Mrs. Molina said. "All teams from all three classes will get the same word to spell. You'll confer among yourselves for thirty seconds and come to an agreement on the spelling. Then you'll write the word, spelled as you think it should be spelled, on a large piece of paper. At the signal, you'll hold up your paper and show it to the judges. Three wrongly spelled words—three 'stingers'—and your team is out."

Whew! Simon could just tell the others how to spell each word, and that's what they'd write down. Cody couldn't ruin the team's chances, after all.

Unless Cody didn't listen to Simon.

Unless Jackson thought Simon was being too bossy, showing off how good he was at everything.

But they wanted to win, too, didn't they?

They wanted to go to the pie buffet and eat Mr. Boone's famous honey pie, too.

Didn't they?

That evening, Simon sat hunched over his parents' huge, heavy dictionary, trying to find the longest word in it to write on the word wall. There were lots of dictionaries in Mrs. Molina's third-grade room, one for every student in the class. But those were special dictionaries for kids. Simon didn't want to find the longest word in an easy kids' dictionary. He wanted to find the longest word in the whole world.

It was slow going. There were so many long words in the dictionary! There had to be an easier way than flipping through the entire dictionary page by page.

He found his parents downstairs in the family room, reading. Whenever his computer scientist father wasn't busy on his laptop, he was reading in his overstuffed armchair. Whenever his musician mother wasn't busy on her cello, she was reading on the couch. If anybody would know the longest word in the world, it would be his parents.

"Mom! Dad!" he shouted. He had learned that he had to shout to get their attention when they were lost in a book.

His thin, balding father looked up.

His thin, red-haired mother looked up.

"What's the longest word in the world?" he asked them.

"The longest English-language word?" his father clarified.

Simon nodded.

"When I was growing up," his mother said, "we were told that it was *antidisestablishmentarianism*."

Simon liked the word already, just from the sound of it. "What does it mean?"

She shrugged. "I have no idea. It's not a word anybody ever says in daily life. It's just famous for being long."

His father chuckled. "*We* were told that the longest word was *pneumonoultramicroscopicsilicovolcanoconiosis.*"

Both Simon and his mother stared. "What?!" they said together.

"And don't ask me what it means, either," his father said. "All I know is that it's the name of some kind of disease."

Simon made his father repeat the word for him until he could say it himself: NEW-mun-oh-ultra-microscopic-SIL-ico-volcano-cone-ee-OH-sis.

It wasn't in the big dictionary, but his father let him look it up on the family-room computer. His parents limited his screen time, but they were always willing to help him find things he needed.

There it was, spelled out on the monitor: a lung disease caused by inhaling tiny particles of volcanic dust.

Simon was going to learn how to spell it even if it took him a whole hour. And then he was going to write it on the word wall tomorrow.

4

The word wall loomed bare and majestic on Wednesday morning, like a ski slope's new snow awaiting the tracks of the day's first skiers.

Simon knew that he and Kelsey would be the day's first spellers.

After the flag salute and morning announcements, he tried beaming a silent message to Kelsey, not that his silent messages to Mrs. Molina ever did any good.

Ask when we can start writing our words on the wall!

He didn't want always to be the one waving his hand in the air with a question.

Either Kelsey got the message or she was already as eager as he was.

"When can we put our words on the word wall?" she asked.

"Any time that I'm not asking you to do something else," Mrs. Molina said. "During *math* time"—she fastened her gaze on Kelsey, who was often reading a book on her lap during math—"I expect you to be paying attention to math. During science time, I expect you to be paying attention to science. But during free time, you may go quietly to the word wall."

"Is it free time now?" Kelsey wanted to know.

"Because it's the first day for the word wall, yes, I'll give you some time now to write on it."

Before Mrs. Molina even finished her sentence, Kelsey was out of her seat, marker in hand.

Simon grabbed his marker and followed her. Half the class—though not Jackson or Cody—dashed over to the word wall, too. Jackson's handwriting was so messy that even if he had written a word on the wall, nobody would have been able to read it.

In his neat, careful printing Simon wrote *pneumonoultramicroscopicsilicovolcanoconiosis.*

Then he waited to let the full impact of his word sink in.

"Look at Simon's word!" he heard one kid say. Other kids—but not Jackson or Cody—left their seats to come gaze at that long string of letters stretching practically all the way across the wall.

"Wow!" another kid exclaimed.

"Is that really a word?" a third kid asked.

Kelsey had stopped copying her own long list of words on the board. "How do you say it?"

Simon was happy to oblige. It was a good thing he had practiced it over and over again last night.

"It's even longer than *supercalifragilistic-expialidocious*!" Kelsey marveled.

"*Supercalifragilisticexpialidocious* isn't a real word," Simon told her. "It's a fake word, made up for the *Mary Poppins* movie."

"Aren't all words made up?" Kelsey demanded. "Your big word—didn't someone have to make *that* up, too?"

Simon had to admit that Kelsey had a point. But his word still seemed more real somehow.

"How many letters does it have?" Annika asked.

"I don't know," Simon said. "I didn't count."

"That's the first thing I'd do!"

That made sense, for math-whiz Annika.

"I think it's silly to make a word be so long," Izzy said. "I could run all the way around

Franklin School—twice!—in the time it takes to say it."

That made sense, too, from running-star Izzy.

Simon was glad that so many of them thought it was an awesome word, even if Jackson hadn't. Jackson was still back in his seat, laughing at some apparently funny thing that Cody had just said.

Simon hoped they weren't laughing at *him*.

Then, as the others drifted away, he wrote a few of his favorite *e* words: *exuberant, exhilarating* (it did have an *a* in the middle—he had checked), and *electrifying*. That was enough words for today. He wasn't going to try to write the *most* words of anybody. That would be too much of a Super Simon thing to do. He wasn't going to cover the whole wall with his words so that there would be no room for words from anybody else.

But he was going to try to write the *best* words of anybody.

He forced himself to stop and read what other kids had written.

Some had written ordinary, everyday words: *chimney, umbrella, microwave*. Bor-ing! Another really good speller, Diego Lopez, had written the names of animals: *chimpanzee, leopard, cheetah*. Those were good words, Simon decided. It was cool that Diego had a theme. His own list of *e* words had a theme, too, but he wasn't planning on sticking with one letter forever.

He was pleased to see that his teammate Annika had a great word: *hypotenuse*. As Annika's fellow math whiz, Simon knew it was a math term, the name of the longest side of a right-angled triangle. Kelsey's teammate Izzy had a good word, too: *kilometer*. Simon knew that races were often measured in kilometers.

Then he let himself look at Kelsey's words. She had written at least twenty. Apparently she wasn't afraid of being called Super Kelsey. Maybe she'd even like that name. Simon wouldn't have minded being called Super Simon if Jackson hadn't laughed after Cody said it.

He ran his eyes down Kelsey's list.

She had started with *supercalifragilisticexpialidocious*. Simon didn't think Mrs. Molina should let a made-up movie word be posted on the word wall.

Extraordinary. She probably thought she was an extraordinary speller. Well, she was awfully good.

Extravagant. Was she copying him by using *e* words?

Viola. That was a kind of musical instrument, like Simon's violin but bigger. Was Kelsey taking private music lessons? Maybe he could tell her about Dr. Lee's secret music language. But he'd rather save it for Jackson's tuba, if Jackson would be willing to go along with him.

Out of the corner of his eye, he saw that Jackson and Cody were still busy talking and laughing.

Then it was time for Mrs. Molina's class to head off for P.E.

Simon pretended he didn't notice Jackson and Cody lining up together.

During language arts time, Mrs. Molina told the class to meet with their spelling teams.

"Just find a quiet corner where you can talk without disturbing the others," she said.

What were they supposed to do in the meeting? Was this the moment for Simon to ask his teammates, *Now, you'll just let me tell you how to spell all the words, right?* He dreaded the thought of how that discussion would go.

But maybe it was better to have it sooner rather than later.

Mrs. Molina continued, "Start by practicing the third-grade spelling words you've been tested on so far this year."

Jackson had already jumped up to claim the couch in the reading nook for their team, another reason for Simon to be grateful that Mrs. Molina had put them together. Simon hurried to occupy the other end of the couch. Cody and Annika plopped themselves down on the oversized beanbag chairs on the floor nearby.

"So now what?" Jackson asked, lolling on the couch, eyes focused on the ceiling.

Simon didn't know how to ask the question he had planned. He just couldn't do it. "I guess we should practice our old spelling words," he said.

Looking around at his teammates, he saw that he was the only one who had remembered to bring his spelling notebook. Not a good sign. But maybe it did show that they'd be willing, even eager, to leave most of the spelling up to him.

"Okay," he said, opening his notebook to the first list of words from back when school started in September. Oh, what pitiful words they were! Words that nobody in the universe could spell wrong!

"*High*," he read out.

"H-i," Jackson said.

Well, maybe somebody could spell it wrong.

Actually, one of the strangest and most wonderful things about the English language was how many words were spelled completely different from how they sounded. Why would *high* have that extra, silent *gh* added on at the end? Why would *taught* and *fought* have that *gh* in the middle? Simon himself got confused by words like that sometimes. The only mistake he had made on a spelling test all year was when he spelled *taught* as *tought* because *taught* rhymed with *fought*. If you stared at words like that too long, you could totally lose your grip on how to spell them, even if you had read them a million times in books.

"Not *hi* like *hello*," Simon explained. "*High* like the opposite of *low*."

This time Jackson spelled it correctly.

Simon read the next word on the list. "*Pencil.*"

Annika got it right.

After two or three dozen easy words— Jackson did spell *scream* as *screem*, and Annika did forget the *u* in *laundry*—Simon noticed that Cody hadn't volunteered to spell a single one. Cody sprawled on his beanbag chair with his eyes closed, asleep or pretending to be.

Should Simon say something or not?

If he did, Cody might say back, "Who made you the teacher?"

If he didn't, wouldn't he be treating Cody like he wasn't even a member of the team at all?

Simon scanned down the list to find the easiest easy word. Which was easier: *full*, *feeling*, or *family*? *Full* was the shortest.

"Hey, Cody," he said, trying to keep his tone casual, "how do you spell *full*?"

A snore came from Cody's direction. Simon knew it had to be a pretend snore. Jackson cracked up.

"Hey, Cody," Jackson asked, "how do you spell *snore*?"

Still pretending to be asleep, Cody made a series of snoring sounds as if he were spelling out the word: five snores, one for each letter.

Annika giggled.

"How do you spell *poop*?" Jackson asked the fake-sleeping Cody.

Four sharp, staccato snores followed.

"I can snore *pee*," Jackson offered, giving three short snores to prove it.

By now Jackson was laughing hysterically. Cody was howling with laughter, too. He had fallen off his beanbag chair onto the floor, and Jackson was starting to tickle him with his feet.

"Jackson, Cody, Annika, Simon!" Mrs. Molina called over to them. "You have officially lost your couch privileges!"

Thanks a lot, Cody! Thanks a lot, Jackson!

"You don't even care whether or not we win, do you?" Simon demanded as they abandoned their comfy couch and squishy beanbag chairs to return to their hard, boring desks. At least Annika was also rolling her eyes in frustration.

Cody didn't answer. Neither did Jackson.

Instead, under his breath, Cody asked Jackson, "How do you spell *Super-Duper-Pooper*?"

Both boys laughed so hard through their chorus of fake snores that finally even Annika started laughing, too.

5

On Saturday afternoon, Simon found himself doing something he would never in his whole life have expected to do.

He was at Annika's house, with Jackson and Cody, trying to teach Annika's dog how to spell.

At the close of the spelling bee teams' second practice on Friday, which for Simon's team was almost as pointless as their "snoring" practice had been, Mrs. Molina had told the teams to try to find some time over the weekend to continue practicing together.

"We could meet at my house," Simon suggested.

Both Jackson and Cody groaned. Simon hoped they were groaning at the idea of having to practice at all, not at the idea of going to his house.

There was a long silence.

"If we did it at my house, we could play video games afterward," Jackson offered.

This time Cody brightened, but Annika said, "I hate video games. If we did it at *my* house, we could teach my dog to spell."

"What's your dog's name?" Cody asked, just as Jackson said, "Dogs can't spell."

"His name is Prime," Annika told Cody, flashing a smile at Simon.

It took Simon a moment to figure out why Annika was grinning specially at him. But then he got it. *Prime*, for *prime number*, a special kind of number that couldn't be divided by any other number except for itself and 1.

"And he's an unusually smart dog, he really is," Annika told Jackson.

"What has he ever done that's so smart?" Jackson wanted to know.

"Lots of things."

"Like what?" Jackson persisted.

"Like, we have a bell hanging from the door-knob on the back door, and he jingles it when he wants to go outside. That's the same thing as talking. Well, practically the same."

Simon didn't think it was the same thing as talking at all.

"And once I almost taught him to count," Annika added.

"*Almost*," Jackson repeated.

"Well, he *might* have learned if I had kept on trying."

"I'm not coming," Jackson said. "Mrs. Molina didn't say we *had* to practice. Your dog can't really learn to spell."

Simon couldn't disagree with that prediction.

But to Simon's surprise, Cody said, "I'm

coming." To Jackson, he said, "You haven't even given him a *chance* to try."

"Okay, I'll come, too," Jackson said grudgingly.

So now the three boys were at Annika's house on a Saturday afternoon, greeted at the door by her friendly brown-and-white beagle.

Simon flinched as Prime jumped on him in welcome. Even a small dog like Prime was a lot bigger than Ferrari the ferret, and at least Ferrari didn't sniff Simon with a doggy snout or lick him with a doggy tongue.

Jackson reached down and gave Prime a friendly pat.

Cody was clearly the one Prime loved most. The dog lay on his back, all four feet in the air, as Cody scratched his exposed belly, apparently finding all of Prime's itchiest spots for rubbing. Simon remembered that Cody lived on a farm outside town and had his own pig,

Mr. Piggins. Maybe Cody also milked cows on the farm, or rode horses, or helped out with other animals.

"You're a good dog! Yes, you are!" Cody kept saying as the dog squirmed in ecstasy.

When they headed into Annika's family room, Prime followed Cody.

When they sat down on Annika's couch, Prime positioned himself by Cody's feet.

"Why does Prime like you so much?" Simon asked, puzzled.

Cody gave a slow smile. "Because I like him, I guess. Isn't that right, boy? Is that why you like me? Because I like you? That's right, I do."

The dog was once again sprawled out on his back, eager for more of Cody's tummy rubs.

After another fifteen minutes of dog scratching, dog patting, paw shaking, and dog-related conversation, no one had yet spelled a single word: no human, no animal. Simon refused to be the first one to mention this fact.

He was grateful when Annika finally said, "So, should we do some spelling?"

"Sure," Simon said, trying to make it sound as if he really didn't care one way or the other.

To Simon's relief, Jackson and Cody didn't offer any protest.

Annika clapped her hand to her head. "I forgot to bring home my spelling notebook! Did any of you remember to bring one?"

The other two boys had come to Annika's empty-handed, so their answer was clear.

Simon unzipped his backpack, set beside him on the floor. "I did," he said.

Jackson and Cody, whose faces had lit up at Annika's confession, now moaned.

Annika said, "Well, we won't be using our school words for Prime anyway. We can't start him with third-grade words right away."

"What words *are* you going to use with Prime?" Simon asked. "And how can he spell them if he can't even talk or write?"

"*We'll* spell words to *him*," Annika explained. "If he understands what we're saying, then we'll know he can spell. Words like *sit*, *stay*, and *lie down*."

That sort of made sense. It wasn't the same thing as real spelling, more like reverse spelling, but Simon was still curious to see if Prime could do it.

"Let me try first," Cody said.

He fished a dog biscuit from the bag Annika had provided. Champion human spellers would have slices of Mr. Boone's honey pie as their reward; champion dog spellers would get Bow Wow brand doggie treats. Annika had also produced a plate of chocolate chip cookies for the team, not as a prize, just as refreshments for the afternoon.

"Prime," Cody commanded. He had stood up from the couch and spoke with an authority Simon had never before heard in his voice. "S-i-t."

It was the first time in any spelling practice that Cody had actually spelled a word.

Prime looked up at Cody expectantly, wagging his tail.

"S-i-t," Cody repeated.

To Simon's great surprise, Prime sat.

"Good dog!" Cody praised him. He gave Prime the biscuit, and Prime gulped it down in one bite.

Even Jackson started clapping for Prime, and Simon joined in.

"See?" Annika beamed. "I told you he was smart!"

"Well," Cody said slowly, giving Prime another friendly rub behind his ears. "Most dogs are going to do whatever they think you

want them to, if they see a treat, and *sit* is the thing they learn first."

He held up a second Bow Wow treat and moved a few feet away. "C-o-m-e," he spelled.

Prime didn't come. Once again, Prime sat.

"See?" Cody said. "He thinks everything is *sit*."

"Okay, maybe he can't spell *yet*," Annika conceded. "That's what we're here for today. To teach him how."

Well, and also to improve their *own* spelling skills for the bee, which was now less than a week away. But Simon didn't say that.

Cody tried again. "C-o-m-e!" As he spelled the word, he bent down and patted his legs, to call Prime to him. Prime bounded over to Cody.

Success?

Impressed, Simon grinned his congratulations at Cody. Cody gave a shy grin in return.

But then Cody shook his head. "Maybe I gave him too much of a clue for that one. Let's try *stay*."

But when Cody said "S-t-a-y" and started to back away, Prime didn't stay. Then again, even when Cody gave him the plain, non-spelled-out "Stay" command, Prime couldn't bear to be left behind and kept bouncing toward Cody.

"That one doesn't count," Annika decided. "He's not really a staying kind of dog."

"L-i-e d-o-w-n" was also a failure. While Prime did respond obediently to the spoken command "Lie down," the string of seven letters was apparently too much.

"Some words are too long for him right now," Annika explained. "Asking him to spell *lie down* is like asking one of us to spell . . ."

"*Pneumonoultramicroscopic*—"

Annika cut Simon off. "Exactly."

"I'll try it just with l-i-e," Cody said. "We can skip d-o-w-n."

Cody spelled the word, pushed Prime into a prone position, and then gave him the Bow Wow treat. Sure enough, after a few tries, Prime had mastered l-i-e.

Or maybe not. When Cody tried going back to s-i-t, Prime got the commands confused. He lay down for s-i-t and sat for l-i-e.

"He's getting tired," Annika explained. "That was a lot of spelling for a dog that never spelled before."

It was a lot of dog biscuits, too. Simon was amazed that a small-sized dog could hold such a large-sized quantity. The four humans had also eaten a considerable share of cookies.

"Well," Jackson said, looking over at the clock on Annika's DVD player. "I told my mom to pick me up at four."

"My dad's picking me up at four, too," Cody said.

Apparently spelling practice was over. The only words that had been successfully drilled in all that time had been s-i-t and c-o-m-e and l-i-e d-o-w-n. Oh, well. Simon had to admit the afternoon had been fun.

It was cool that Cody had a talent for animals that Simon hadn't known about. You didn't know everything about somebody from what he was like at school. When it came to animals, Cody was Super Cody.

"You're great with animals," Simon said to Cody as he stuffed his unopened spelling book into his backpack.

"Thanks," Cody said, sounding as if he meant it.

The doorbell rang.

"It's probably my dad," Cody said. "He might be a bit early."

But when Annika opened the door, there stood Kelsey and Izzy.

"I just got back from running," said Izzy.

"And I just got back from the library," said Kelsey.

"And we thought we'd stop by," Izzy continued.

"To see if you wanted to go for a walk," Kelsey finished.

Then, for the first time, Kelsey noticed the boys. She looked from Annika to Simon, Jackson, and Cody, and then back at Annika again.

"We were practicing for the spelling bee," Annika explained.

"Oh," Kelsey said, her tone suddenly icy. Her glistening eyes and lifted chin clearly spelled the word *traitor*.

But it wasn't Annika's fault that she had been assigned to a different spelling team from her friends. And Simon would hardly call stuffing Prime full of Bow Wow treats "practicing for the spelling bee." He was willing to bet Kelsey's team was practicing that weekend, too, and that *they* would be spelling practice words *themselves*, not just coaxing someone's dog to recognize spelled-out words.

"Sorry for interrupting," Kelsey said haughtily. "Come on, Izzy, let's go."

She turned on her heel and left. Izzy shot Annika an apologetic grin and then trailed after Kelsey.

Was competition going to cause as much trouble for Annika and Kelsey as it already seemed to be causing for Simon and Jackson? And Simon and Jackson were even on the same team!

As soon as the door shut behind her friends, Annika sighed. Then she gave a little shrug, as if shaking off Kelsey's attempt at a quarrel.

"Don't mind Kelsey," she said. "She gets like this when she really wants to win something."

That was plainly true.

Simon could understand. He wanted to win, too. But as he looked over at Jackson and Cody rolling on the floor with Prime, who was done with spelling for the day, he wondered if somehow he had already lost.

6

By Monday the word wall in Mrs. Molina's room was filling up nicely.

As Kelsey was adding her words on the far edge of the wall, Simon tried to find an empty place to add more words in his small, precise writing, so different from Jackson's unreadable scrawl.

Delicious.

Delectable.

Delightful.

Just as he was about to write *delirious*, Mr. Boone came buzzing into Mrs. Molina's room.

Mr. Boone wasn't wearing a bee outfit, though Simon expected to see him appear any day in black-and-yellow stripes complete with gauzy wings.

Instead, Mr. Boone was wearing a ruffled apron, printed with pictures of different pieces of pie. In one hand, he carried what Simon recognized as a flour sifter. In the other hand, he carried a long wooden rolling pin. On his head was a tall white chef's hat with bunches of fake bright red cherries pinned on the top.

"Good morning, third graders!" Mr. Boone boomed.

"Good morning, Mr. Boone!" the class shouted back.

Mrs. Molina smiled weakly. She always seemed a bit ill at ease when Mr. Boone's larger-than-life energy exploded into her calm, orderly classroom.

"How are a-l-l of y-o-u doing with your . . ."

He trailed off midsentence as his gaze fell

upon the spelling wall. He staggered back a few steps as if overcome by the sight of so many words all in one place.

"I guess I can answer my own question!" he said heartily.

Approaching the wall, where Simon and Kelsey were still standing, markers in hand, he started reading out words at random.

"*Microwave.* A most useful device, but not good for making honey pie. *Extraordinary.* Precisely the word I would use to describe the taste of my honey pie. *Delicious* and *delectable.* Ditto! The person who wrote those words must have had my honey pie in mind when he or she wrote them. Oh, and here's one of my favorites!"

Mr. Boone began singing "Supercalifragilisticexpialidocious" from *Mary Poppins*, loudly and off-key.

So maybe you didn't have to be good at

everything, or at least good at music, to be a principal.

Or maybe Mr. Boone was just trying to be funny. Certainly everyone in the class was in stitches, and even Mrs. Molina was smiling a real smile now.

Then Mr. Boone squinted at the first word Simon had written last week. "Oh my goodness!"

He started trying to sound out Simon's longest long word.

"Puh-new-monomono-monomono-ultra-something. No, let me start over again. Puh-new-mono-ultra . . . volanco?"

The class laughed even harder.

Simon felt a tingle of pleasure that it was *his* long word that was causing Mr. Boone so much hilarious trouble.

"I give up!" Mr. Boone declared. "Who can help me out here?"

Still standing by the board, marker in hand, Simon said the word as fast and as perfectly as he could, one syllable spilling out after another, each one in place.

When he was done, Mr. Boone whacked his sifter and his rolling pin together in applause, and the rest of the class clapped along with him.

If only Mr. Boone would come to their class every day! Maybe Jackson wouldn't blame Simon so much for being Super Simon.

"Now," Mr. Boone said, "I have a few words of my own that I want to add to your wall, if I can remember how to spell them. May I?"

He reached out for Simon's green marker and handed him his sifter in exchange. In a blank space on the board, in large green letters, he wrote *PRACTICE*.

Simon hoped that Jackson and Cody were paying attention.

CHIMNEY

exhilarating   umbrella
elating   extravagant
electrifying
          extraordinary
VIOLA
...percalifrag... ...rialidocious
          ...crowave
...pey ...oultramicro-
...rful ...covolcanoconiosis
          gerbil
...anzee   etcetera

Then he borrowed Kelsey's orange marker, letting her hold his rolling pin. With Kelsey's marker, he wrote *TEAMWORK*.

Simon didn't like that word as much.

Then in the biggest letters of all, he wrote one more, very short word, just three letters, short enough that even Prime could spell it: *PIE*.

The class cheered.

Mr. Boone returned Simon's and Kelsey's markers and collected his baking implements.

Whistling "Supercalifragilisticexpialidocious" perfectly in tune this time, he headed out the door.

After school that day, instead of hurrying home to practice violin and search in his parents' dictionary for some new mega-cool words for the word wall, Simon peeked into the third-grade classroom next to Mrs. Molina's. If the spelling bee words could be drawn from any class's word wall, it was time to check out the walls in Mr. Knox's and Mrs. Rodriguez-Haramia's rooms.

A thought popped into his head. The kids in Mrs. Rodriguez-Haramia's class would have to be good spellers just to spell their teacher's hyphenated name.

Mr. Knox, much younger and cheerier than Mrs. Molina, looked up from his desk.

"May I help you?" he asked in a friendly way.

Simon found himself feeling shy. "I'm from Mrs. Molina's room. I was wondering . . . would it be okay . . . would you mind if I looked at your spelling wall? Just for a minute?"

Mr. Knox chuckled. "Someone else from your class was here on Friday. A girl who had her spelling notebook with her. Kacey, I think her name was. Or Kelly?"

Kelsey!

That sneak! That spy!

Then Simon remembered that sneaking and spying were exactly what he himself had come to do.

"Did you let her look?" Simon asked.

"Sure I did," Mr. Knox replied. "I figure, the whole point of a spelling bee is to get kids excited about spelling, right?"

Simon couldn't agree more.

As Mr. Knox turned back to grading papers, Simon studied this new word wall. Someone in Mr. Knox's class had also written *supercalifragilisticexpialidocious*. Didn't anyone else care that it was just a fake movie word? No one had written Simon's longest of all long words. He saw three hard words, all in the same handwriting, presumably from their class's best speller: *pathetic, paranoid, peculiar*. Simon wrote them down in his spelling notebook; Kelsey wasn't the only one who carried a spelling notebook everywhere.

"Thanks!" Simon told Mr. Knox when he was done.

"Good luck at the bee!" Mr. Knox said. "Though, as I'm sure you know, practice counts a lot more than luck does. Practice and team-work."

Simon noticed that Mr. Boone had written the same three words—*PRACTICE*, *TEAM-WORK*, and *PIE*—on Mr. Knox's word wall, too. He wished his class had been the only one Mr. Boone visited. Maybe Mr. Boone had sung the song from *Mary Poppins* loudly and badly for Mr. Knox's class, too.

But he knew that Mr. Boone hadn't botched the pronunciation of *pneumonoultramicro-scopicsilicovolcanoconiosis* for them.

Thanks to Simon, that was a special, funny thing he had done for Mrs. Molina's class alone.

That evening after dinner, once Simon had finished his homework, practiced violin, and found some more words for the word wall (*obstinate, obelisk*), Simon and his parents set up their favorite game on the kitchen table: Scrabble.

In Scrabble, you drew little wooden letter tiles and had to make words out of them. The hard thing about it was that you couldn't just plop your word on the board anywhere; with the exception of the very first word, it had to link up with some word already there.

Each letter in your word was worth a certain number of points: from one point for common letters like e, a, and r up to ten points for the most special letters, q and z. Where you placed your word on the board mattered, too. You could double or triple the value of a letter or a word depending on where you put it.

Simon loved the challenge of Scrabble. But the most fun thing about it was watching his quiet, kind, gentle, book-loving parents turn into the world's worst cutthroat, competitive fiends.

"Okay, you two," his father crowed partway through the game as he began laying his letter tiles down on the board. "Beat this!"

His father spelled out *quilt*, with the ten-point *q* falling on a triple-letter space, so earning thirty points for that one letter alone.

"That's nothin'," his mother shot back.

On another part of the board, using an *m* that was already there, his mother spelled out the word *mailbox*. Its seven letters meant that she used up all her letter tiles in one fell swoop, a feat worth an additional fifty bonus points. Plus, *x* was already worth eight points all by itself, *and* her word fell on a triple-word space. One hundred and four points!

Both his parents looked his way.

"Your turn, squirt!" his father taunted.

"Can you spell *pitiful*?" his mother jeered.

Simon studied his letter tiles. He had horrible letters: six vowels, with just one consonant, *s*. No letter he had was worth more than one point. *Pitiful* was right.

Then he saw: he could add *es* to his mother's word *mailbox*. The *s* would fall on the triple-*word* space, so he'd get triple for the whole nine-letter word. He could count *x* three times, and get sixty points total. It wasn't as big as his mom's score, but all he had done was add two measly letters!

With a flourish, he put his two tiles in place.

"Ratfink!" his father moaned.

"Stinker!" his mother wailed.

Simon beamed.

Then his father clapped him on the back, and his mother leaned over to give him a smothering hug.

7

Jackson hadn't invited Simon over since the Galaxy Warriors quarrel, and Simon had been afraid to ask. But Jackson's mom texted Simon's mom to set up something after school on Tuesday at Jackson's house. Mrs. Myers picked the boys up at school to drive them home.

"You two are awfully quiet," she commented.

As if to prove her point, neither boy replied. In the backseat of the car, Jackson gazed out the window to his left, and Simon gazed out the window to his right.

"I remember how the two of you would be in

gales of giggles playing that game you made up with the stuffed animals. What did you call it? You gave it some kind of name."

"Bird War," Simon answered, since Jackson was still staring out the window.

"That's right," Jackson's mom said. "And remember that time . . ."

Simon knew exactly which time she meant. Jackson did, too, because he grinned at Simon and spoke for the first time on the ride.

"The police pulled you over!"

"I was swerving a little bit, on purpose, on this empty stretch of country road with no other cars around anywhere, trying to get more birds to fall off. I loved how you both got so hysterical whenever one of them toppled. And then that police car appeared out of nowhere!"

"The siren was so cool," Jackson said. "And the flashing lights! My mom—busted!"

"Thank goodness he didn't give me a ticket," his mom said. "He took one look at the two of you in the backseat, with those heaps of stuffed birds flung everywhere, and I think he felt sorry for me."

It had only been last year, but it seemed so long ago now.

"Okay," Mrs. Myers said as she drove into their three-car garage. "At least we made it home today without getting the police involved."

Inside their big farm-style kitchen, she set out cheese, crackers, and grapes for a snack.

"I'm glad Mrs. Molina put you two Bird Warriors on the same spelling team. It's nice when friends can be on the same side."

"Yes, it is," Simon said politely.

Jackson was starting to look sullen again, cramming a cracker into his mouth as if to avoid having to talk about the spelling bee.

"Do you want me to quiz you on any words to help you get ready?" Mrs. Myers asked. "The bee is just three days away."

"No thanks," Simon said. He couldn't imagine Jackson would want to drill spelling words when they could be playing video games.

"Simon can already spell every word in the universe," Jackson said, talking with his mouth still full. It didn't come out sounding like a compliment.

Simon shook his head in protest. There were probably millions of words he couldn't spell; he made a mental note to find out how many words there were in the English language.

Jackson's mother gave her son a quizzical look. "Simon's spelling talents will be a big help on Friday, I'm sure!" she said brightly.

"Yeah," Jackson said, not even trying to hide his sarcasm. "It can be like one big long game of Simon Says. Simon says, Take two giant steps. Simon says, Take two baby steps. Simon says, This is how you spell *dog*. Simon says, This is how you spell *cat*."

Simon remembered another game they used to play. Back in first grade, Jackson had complained about the unfairness of having a game named after Simon, when no game was named after him. So they had invented Jackson Says. In Jackson Says, they didn't tell each other to do things like hop on one foot or turn around twice. It had to be something gross: *Jackson says, Pick your nose. Jackson says, Squish a bug.*

Simon wondered if Jackson remembered that, too.

"Now, Jackson," his mother said. "Don't you want your team to win?"

"Sure," Jackson said.

But he didn't sound as if he meant it.

Upstairs in Jackson's room, Ferrari seemed a lot more overjoyed to see Simon than his owner did. Released from his cage, the ferret jumped

from Jackson's neck to Simon's and settled there like a furry scarf.

Simon remembered how much Annika's dog had adored Cody. Then he had some uncomfortable thoughts.

Would Ferrari, too, want to scamper after Cody everywhere, as Prime had?

Had Cody already come over to Jackson's house to play Galaxy Warriors with Ferrari on his lap?

He pushed those thoughts away.

"We could try teaching Ferrari to spell," Simon suggested.

He kept his tone joking, but he was actually serious. Could Ferrari be trained to follow some simple spelled-out commands? Were ferrets as smart as dogs, or smarter, or not as smart? Maybe different kinds of animals were smart in different ways, just like different kids.

"Ha ha," Jackson said. He didn't sound

amused. "Do you want to know what I think about spelling? I'm s-i-c-k of it. I don't l-o-v-e school the way you do."

"I bet Ferrari's as smart as Prime," Simon said, trying to turn the conversation in a friendly direction.

"Smart isn't everything," Jackson shot back.

Was Simon supposed to apologize for being smart? He couldn't help being smart!

But maybe he *could* help winning all the time.

"Do you want to play Galaxy Warriors or Amphibian Apocalypse?" Simon asked hesitantly.

Jackson shrugged. Then he popped Galaxy Warriors into the game system and handed Simon one of the controllers.

This time, Simon was determined not to win. This wasn't like playing Scrabble with his parents, where you could try your hardest to cream the other person and then end the game with a hug and a smile.

As Satu this time, Simon purposely fired his fireballs when he knew Xalik was ready to leap up and dodge them.

He deliberately didn't duck out of the way of Xalik's lasers.

He made sure to stop firing when he saw Xalik needed to recharge his laser beam.

Just as Xalik scored another hit, Jackson clicked off the game. He threw his controller onto the bed, hard enough that it bounced off the bedspread and onto the carpeted floor.

"You're letting me win."

Simon felt himself flush.

"No, I'm not. I'm just . . . I just got distracted. Anyone can get distracted."

Jackson glared at him with Xalik's laser-beam eyes. "You never get distracted."

"Yes, I do!"

"No, you don't!"

"Jackson," Simon pleaded. "You get mad if I win. You get mad if I lose. What am I supposed to do?"

Jackson shot another piercing laser gaze Simon's way. "You're so smart, you figure it out."

8

Mrs. Molina gave the spelling teams another chance to practice on Wednesday. This time Kelsey's team was cozily settled in the couch area, so Simon's team had to carry their chairs to a different corner of the room. Simon bet Kelsey's team wouldn't lose their couch privileges for misbehaving.

"Remember," Simon told his teammates, "Mrs. Molina said the judges can ask us to spell words from the word walls, too."

Maybe that would motivate them to work a little harder. At least now, with the spelling bee just two days away, no one was fake snoring yet.

"I've been checking the word walls in the other third-grade rooms," Simon continued. He had visited Mr. Knox and Mrs. Rodriguez-Haramia twice now. "I made a list of their hardest words. Do you want to see it?"

No one looked particularly eager.

"*Kelsey* has been secretly checking their walls, too," Simon added. In addition to the report from Mr. Knox, he had seen Kelsey leaving Mrs. Rodriguez-Haramia's room yesterday just as he was arriving. The two of them had glared at each other.

Jackson and Cody still looked unimpressed.

Annika fiddled with one of her long blond braids. "I wish Kelsey and Izzy weren't on a different team," she said. "I'll be sad if we lose to them, but I'll be just as sad if they lose to us."

"Don't be," Jackson told her, his competitive

spirit finally roused. "You have to root for your own team the most. That's just how it is with teams. Do you want Kelsey's team to get all the pie, or us?"

Yes! Now it felt as if Simon and Jackson were finally on the same side. Hooray for the power of pie!

"Let's think of a cool name for our team," Jackson said, on a roll now.

"Something that starts with *S*, then Spellers," Simon suggested. He knew better than to suggest Simon's Spellers.

"How about Special Spellers?" Annika asked.

Even though Annika was trying to stir up some team spirit now, Simon wondered if she'd tell Kelsey that their team was going to have a name, so that Kelsey's team could try to come up with an even better one. It wouldn't be hard to find a better name than Special Spellers.

"Wait," Simon said as a name popped into his head. "Spectacular Spellers."

A spectacular team name should have a spectacular word in it.

He was glad when Cody and Jackson both nodded.

"We should have a team mascot, too," Cody said.

At the same instant, both Cody and Annika shouted, "Prime!"

Then Jackson said, "T-shirts!"

Ten minutes later, after a debate about whether the team name should be printed on the back or on the front (back won), and whether they should try to put Prime's picture on it somewhere (consensus: too hard to do), they had plans for yellow-and-black team T-shirts. Jackson said his mom knew an inexpensive place that could make T-shirts in an hour.

Mrs. Molina announced that practice time was over.

Once again, Simon's team hadn't practiced a single word.

At least now, though, they were acting as if they cared about the spelling bee. That counted for something.

But from over in the couch area, Simon had heard Kelsey drilling her team.

Real, hard, actual practice counted for even more.

Simon had his violin lesson that afternoon, on Wednesday instead of Monday, because Dr. Lee had been out of town playing with her chamber music ensemble.

"How is everything going with the spelling bee?" she asked him. "Did it take place yet?"

"It's on Friday," Simon told her. "We have to do it in teams."

Dr. Lee asked, "You don't care for teams?"

"No," Simon told her. "I'm not a team kind

of person to start with, and our team has the worst speller in the class, plus this girl who's rooting as much for our enemy team as she is for us, plus my best friend, Jackson, who isn't really my best friend anymore, because now he gets mad at me all the time if I win at anything and gets even madder if I lose on purpose, so it's . . . hard."

"I see," Dr. Lee said.

From her tall bookcase, filled with musical scores and recordings, she selected two CDs. She inserted the first one into the portable player she kept on the table next to the piano.

Slow, sad, almost unbearably lovely music started playing, just one solo violin, all by itself.

After a minute or two, Dr. Lee said, "Johann Sebastian Bach. Violin Sonata Number One in G Minor."

Simon knew it had to be in a minor key; minor keys were the keys of sadness.

Dr. Lee removed that CD and inserted the second one.

The next piece opened with a full orchestra playing a more lively, energetic, joyous piece. One violin soared above the rest, sweet and pure, but supported by the glorious music of the rest of the strings.

"Wolfgang Amadeus Mozart," Dr. Lee said. "Concerto Number One in A Major."

Major keys were the keys of happiness.

Simon knew right away what she wanted him to be hearing, but she spelled it out for him anyway.

"It's beautiful to hear the violin playing alone, but it's also beautiful to hear it playing with others. Perhaps even more beautiful?"

Simon wanted to tell Dr. Lee, *Spelling is different from music.*

He wanted to say, *What if the other people don't really like playing with YOU?*

He wanted to ask, *Do you think Jackson and I can ever be friends again the way we used to?*

"There is a proverb, a wise saying," Dr. Lee said. " 'You travel fastest if you travel alone.' "

That sounded right.

" 'But you travel farthest if you travel together.' Now let me hear a D major scale, two octaves, and the major and minor arpeggios, please."

On Thursday there was hardly any room left on Mrs. Molina's word wall for Simon to add his latest treasures, but he managed to squeeze them in.

Hydrophobia. Fear of water.

Claustrophobia. Fear of closed-in spaces.

Acrophobia. Fear of heights.

His mother had helped him find a list of words online, all names of fears that apparently were common enough that people had bothered to give them long fancy names. How satisfying they were to say!

After lunch, he saw that Kelsey had spent some free time hunting on the classroom computer for *phobia* words, too. Copycat! In her loopy printing, on the word wall, he saw *agoraphobia*, which he remembered was fear of open spaces.

He hurried over to the wall to write *arachnophobia*. Fear of spiders.

"All right, class, time for language arts," Mrs. Molina said. "Simon, back to your seat."

As Simon hastily finished his word and returned to his desk, Mr. Boone poked his head into the doorway. Mrs. Molina sighed at the interruption.

"Tomorrow is our big day for all you

champion spellers," Mr. Boone greeted the class. He was wearing his ruffled pie-baking apron and tall chef's hat again; this time he had left behind his sifter and rolling pin, but he had a streak of powdery white flour on one cheek.

"When do the winners get their pie?" someone called out to him.

Mr. Boone gave a big grin as he bounded into Mrs. Molina's room.

"The winning teams from each grade will report to the pie buffet after the bee tomorrow!" he boomed. "With pie for everyone else sometime next week!"

The class cheered.

Once again, Mr. Boone pretended to faint at the sight of the word wall, now so crammed full of words there was barely space to write *to, too,* or *two.* As a sign of respect, he removed his white chef's hat and held it solemnly over his heart.

Hat still in hand, Mr. Boone approached the wall and examined it more closely. He looked at Simon's *phobia* words on the bottom left corner of the wall. Then Mr. Boone's gaze roamed across the board to the far right-hand edge, where Kelsey had started adding *phobia* words of her own.

"I think maybe I can find room for one more word," he said.

Beneath Simon's list—not Kelsey's, Simon was pleased to note—Mr. Boone wrote a very long word in very small letters.

Then he vanished back into the hallway as suddenly as he had appeared.

Simon and Kelsey ran over to the board at the same time.

Sesquipedalphobia.

They exchanged puzzled glances.

Mrs. Molina joined them, squinting at the word.

"What does it mean?" they asked her together.

"I don't believe I know," she said. "I doubt it's in our classroom dictionaries, either. Why don't the two of you look it up online?"

Simon and Kelsey raced to the computer.

Kelsey did the typing as Simon dictated to her what he tried to remember of the spelling.

"The fear of long words!" they both read aloud, and burst out laughing.

Simon now knew what he had suspected all along. Mr. Boone was indeed a very good speller, as a principal ought to be: a good speller *and* a good pie baker, although Simon wouldn't know that until tomorrow, *if* he got the chance to taste Mr. Boone's famous honey pie.

What if he didn't? What if Kelsey and her team, or some super spellers from one of the other two classes, were the ones tasting it instead?

He wondered if there was a long, fancy *pho-bia* word for fear of losing.

And with Jackson acting the way he had lately, maybe there needed to be a long, fancy *phobia* word for fear of winning, too.

9

Simon's spelling team caused a sensation when they arrived at school on Friday morning in their matching T-shirts: yellow shirts with SPECTACULAR SPELLERS emblazoned in big black letters on the back. Jackson's mom had dropped the shirts off at everybody's house the night before.

Then Simon saw Kelsey's team standing on the other side of the blacktop, wearing *their* T-shirts: black shirts with SUPERCALIFRAGILISTIC SPELLERS written in yellow.

Kelsey's team name had a longer word.

If it really *was* a word.

Which it wasn't.

Annika had been standing with Simon, Jackson, and Cody. Now she looked over at Kelsey and Izzy with longing in her eyes.

Simon had to ask her, "Did you tell Kelsey about our T-shirts?"

"Not really." Annika was a terrible liar. "Well, sort of." She tugged on one of her braids. "I mean, I couldn't let Kelsey and Izzy's team have no T-shirts at all!"

Simon wasn't really mad. He wondered if Jackson would have done the same for him if they had been the friends assigned to rival teams. Then he thought how much fun it would have been to have Kelsey on their team, someone else who loved spelling as much as he did.

No other team in Mrs. Molina's class had thought of T-shirts, but he saw some kids from Mr. Knox's class with SPELLING BEE BUZZERS shirts, and some kids from Mrs. Rodriguez-Haramia's class with shirts that said KILLER BEES. Simon could imagine his parents choosing a name like that if they ever joined a Scrabble team.

It was hard to concentrate on math, science, and art that morning. At least the third-grade teachers had declared the word walls officially closed. So Simon didn't need to torment himself wondering what new words might appear that he didn't know or couldn't spell. He knew he had missed some anyway. He hadn't checked the word walls every single day. Even if he had, it was hard to notice every single word that had been added to those crowded surfaces.

Finally, after lunch, it was time for the bee to begin.

The third graders, grouped by teams, filed into the cafeteria; the fourth and fifth graders had already had their bees in the morning.

Simon saw his parents sitting together in one of the rows of folding chairs set up for the audience. They could take time off during the day for special school events, though Simon's mom missed a lot of evening events for cello performances.

Annika's parents and Cody's parents weren't there, but Simon spotted Kelsey's mom in the center of the front row, camera on her lap, presumably ready to film Kelsey's victory. Jackson's dad was at work, but his mom, seated next to Simon's mom, gave both boys a friendly wave.

Simon's parents beamed over at him. He was glad they had both come. But seeing them looking his way with such pride in their eyes made his stomach clench even more with wanting to win.

The four-member teams lined up in order around three sides of the room, beneath their posted team numbers, eighteen teams in all. Kelsey's team was 13. Simon's team was 16. At the rear of the room the three teachers and Mr. Boone sat at a long table, with a microphone, a timer, and word lists set out in front of them.

Someone from each team was in charge of carrying the large pad of paper and a handful of markers. Jackson had theirs. Simon had made sure to let someone else be the one to carry it so he wouldn't look bossy before the spelling even began.

His team hadn't done very well with Mr. Boone's first word on the word wall: *PRACTICE*. But he was going to do his best at *TEAMWORK*. And then maybe they'd be rewarded with *PIE*.

"Are you ready, spellers?" Mr. Boone asked.

He looked like a normal principal, wearing a jacket and tie. Simon had thought today might be the day Mr. Boone would finally come dressed in a bee costume, but maybe he couldn't find one in his size. Or maybe Mr. Boone was trying to let the spellers know that the time for silliness was past and the time for seriousness had begun.

"Yes!" all the teams shouted in response to his question.

In the bare cafeteria, their voices had an unsettling echo. It felt scarier and more real now, as they stood huddled together waiting to hear the words read out that would determine their fate.

"Word number one," Mr. Knox said. "*Listen*. In order to do well, it is important that you *listen* to instructions. *Listen*."

At first Simon thought Mr. Knox was giving them a final piece of advice for how to succeed in the spelling bee, but then he realized that *listen* was the word to be spelled. Each word would be spoken with careful pronunciation, then used in a sentence, and then spoken again.

Simon forced himself to let one of his teammates speak first.

"L-i-s-t-e-n," Annika whispered so that the team next to them wouldn't hear.

Jackson nodded. Cody—imitating Jackson?— nodded, too.

After Simon's nod, Annika wrote the word on the top sheet of paper. When the timer beeped, Jackson held it up for the teachers to see. Looking around the room, Simon saw that all eighteen teams had spelled it correctly. It would have been pretty pathetic if they hadn't.

The next few words were harder—*society*, *government*, and *experiment*. Two teams got a stinger with *government* (they left out the first *n*) and another with *experiment* (they put *a* instead of *i*).

After five more third-grade spelling words,

no teams had been eliminated. Lots of teams had stingers now, but Simon's team and Kelsey's team still had a perfect record. A team from Mrs. Rodriguez-Haramia's class had two stingers: one more, and they'd be out.

The words became harder. Word-wall words at last! The audience now clapped after each round, both to congratulate the teams that had gotten the answer right and to praise the effort of the teams that had gotten it wrong.

"*Calendar*," Mrs. Molina read. "I turned the page of the *calendar* from March to April. *Calendar*."

"C-a-l-e-n-d-e-r?" Jackson guessed.

"C-a-l-a-n-d-e-r?" Annika guessed.

Cody didn't ever bother to guess.

"It's c-a-l-e-n-d-a-r," Simon corrected. He was sure about that one.

No one raised any objection to Simon's spelling. Annika had written down all their words so far. This time, for the first time, Simon was the one who wrote the word on the large pad to display.

"Stinger for teams 4, 7, 9, 11, and 13," Mrs. Rodriguez-Haramia called out. Team 13 was Kelsey's team: their first stinger. Jackson started to cheer, but Annika silenced him with a stony look. Kelsey's lip trembled, and her cheeks flamed. Simon couldn't help feeling bad for her; he would have felt just as terrible if the stinger had been his.

For the next three words, Simon didn't even bother to consult the others. It was faster just to tell them how to spell *principal* (Mr. Boone beamed), *agoraphobia* (Simon's word, yay!), and *weird* (short, but tempting to spell it wrong, as you'd think it followed the *i*-before-*e* rule, and it didn't). Only six teams of the original eighteen were left now, including Kelsey's team 13 and Simon's team 16.

Simon's team had yet to have their first stinger. But Jackson was starting to look dangerously sulky as Simon told them how to spell *separate*. He knew it had an *a* in the middle because it was "a rat" of a word to spell.

"What about teamwork?" Jackson asked. "I thought we were supposed to be a team."

What about practice, Simon wanted to reply, *which none of you wanted to do for the last two weeks? What about winning?*

"How do you think we should spell it?" Simon asked Jackson, keeping his tone polite.

"S-e-p-e-r-a-t-e," Jackson told him, jutting his chin up.

Did Jackson really think that, or was he just getting sick of being bossed around by Super Simon?

The seconds were ticking down.

"Annika? Cody?" Simon asked, itching to pick up the marker to write.

"What Simon said," Annika said.

Cody gave his usual shrug.

"Okay," Jackson said, heaving an irritated sigh. "Everyone always has to do what Simon says, just like in the stupid little kid game, right?"

As Mrs. Molina gave the three-second warning, Jackson grabbed the marker from Simon and scrawled the word in angry, jagged strokes. He held up their pad just as the thirty-second timer beeped.

Thank goodness Annika had weighed in on Simon's side!

"Stingers for teams 2 and 16," Mrs. Molina said.

Team 16! Simon's team!

He heard a low murmur rising from the audience, but he didn't let himself look out at his parents to see their reaction.

That couldn't be right.

"What?" Simon called out.

"The correct spelling is s-e-p-*a*-r-a-t-e," Mrs. Molina said.

"That's what we wrote!" Simon protested. "That's how we spelled it."

Mrs. Molina walked over from the teachers' table to inspect the sign Jackson had displayed. For the first time, Simon looked at it, too.

It said *seperate*.

Shocked, he glared at Jackson. How could Jackson have done this? Were they a team or not?

But Jackson, too, had a stunned look on his face.

"That's an *a*," Jackson said in a choked voice, pointing at what Simon, and apparently Mrs. Molina, thought looked exactly like an *e*. "You just can't read my writing! I wrote *a*. Really, I did. That's what we all agreed on, and that's what I wrote. You have to believe me."

"I'm sorry," Mrs. Molina said, her voice full of genuine regret. "But we have to go by what the word looks like, not what you meant it to look like."

She seemed to know that this wasn't a good time to remind Jackson about the importance of legible handwriting.

As Mrs. Molina headed back to the teachers' table, Jackson seemed close to tears.

10

"If we lose the spelling bee, it'll be my dumb fault," Jackson muttered. "Simon's always right; I'm always wrong. That's just how it is."

"That's not true!" Simon protested.

Mr. Knox read out the next word. Simon put up his hand to signal the others to be quiet so he could focus with all his might on what Mr. Knox was saying.

"*Responsibility*. It is important to take *responsibility* for your mistakes. *Responsibility*."

Simon recognized it from the word wall in Mrs. Rodriguez-Haramia's room.

He beamed another of his silent messages to his teammates: *Please, somebody who isn't me, spell it right!*

Annika shook her head, signaling cluelessness.

Cody didn't even bother to do that.

Jackson stared straight ahead, eyes glittering, as if willing himself not to cry.

Simon couldn't stand it any longer. Super Simon cared about winning the spelling bee more than anything else in the world. But it didn't matter anymore to plain-real-kid Simon, to Jackson's best friend Simon.

"Three-second warning," Mr. Knox called out.

"R-e-s-p-o-n-s-a-b-i-l-i-t-y," Simon wrote.

Hands trembling, he held it up for the teachers to see.

"Stingers for teams 5, 7, 13, and 16," Mr. Knox announced.

At least Kelsey's team had gotten a second stinger this round, too.

"Wait," Annika said. "*We* got another stinger? *You* got it wrong?"

Simon nodded. He felt himself flushing.

"That's okay," Cody said, trying to comfort him. "Only two teams got it right. I might be good with animals, but you're great with spelling. You got more words right than the rest of us put together."

Somehow Cody's kindness made Simon feel even worse.

Jackson had yet to speak. His eyes met Simon's and held Simon's gaze.

He knows, Simon thought.

Would Jackson be mad at him all over again, even madder than he had been when Simon lost the Galaxy Warriors game on purpose?

Jackson gave him a shaky smile.

Simon gave him a shaky smile back.

"*Foreign*," Mrs. Rodriguez-Haramia called out. "It is useful to learn how to speak a *foreign* language. *Foreign*."

Only four teams were left now: Simon's team, Kelsey's team, a team from Mr. Knox's class, and one from Mrs. Rodriguez-Haramia's class.

Simon wasn't sure about this one. He remembered from the word wall that it had one of those unexpected consonants in the middle of it: f-o-r-e-i-g-h-n? "I think it's f-o-r-e-i-g-h-n." Or maybe it just had a *g* and not an *h*? "No, f-o-r-e-i-g-n," he corrected.

No one disagreed.

He wrote it down and held his breath as Mrs. Rodriguez-Haramia called out a stinger for Mr. Knox's remaining team.

"*Forfeit*," Mr. Knox read next. "A team that breaks the rules will *forfeit* the match. *Forfeit*."

His teammates shrugged. More confident this time, Simon wrote down the correct spelling.

It was another one of those words that broke the *i*-before-*e* rule.

Stinger for Mrs. Rodriguez-Haramia's remaining team.

There were just two teams left now: Simon's team and Kelsey's.

"*Trough*," Mrs. Molina read. "The pig eats his supper from his *trough*. *Trough*."

Simon didn't remember that one from the word walls. But he knew he had missed some of the shorter words, as his eyes always went to the longer, fancier ones.

He hesitated.

"T-r-o-f-f," Annika suggested.

"That's what it sounds like," Jackson agreed.

"No," Simon said. "There has to be some trick to it, because the words are getting harder now."

It was probably one of those puzzling *gh*-words. Or was it a *ph*-word? The *f* sound was sometimes spelled *gh*, but it was sometimes spelled *ph*. *Graph. Triumph.* The boy's name *Joseph.* They had already been asked a hard word with a *g* in it. The teachers probably wouldn't pick a hard *g*-word twice. The trick would be that this was a *ph*-word instead.

"It's t-r-o-u-p-h," Simon decided.

He was about to write it down, when Cody spoke in his soft voice. "No."

The other three all stared at him.

"It's t-r-o-u-g-h," Cody said. "It ends in *gh*, not *ph*."

"Which is it?" Jackson asked Simon.

Now Simon wasn't sure. He wasn't sure of much of anything right now.

T-r-o-u-p-h? or t-r-o-u-g-h? Both sounded equally right. Or equally wrong.

Then he remembered. Cody lived on a farm. Cody even had a pet pig. Cody's pig probably ate out of that thing, however it was spelled.

Simon picked up the marker.

"T-r-o-u," he wrote. Then he finished it: "g-h."

This time, for the first time, Cody held up the paper for the teachers to see.

And this time, for the first time, Mr. Boone gave the verdict, instead of having one of the three teachers take turns doing it.

Mr. Boone checked the two signs, one held up by Simon's team and one by Kelsey's.

T-r-o-u-p-h for Kelsey's team.

T-r-o-u-g-h for Simon's team.

Only one of them could be correct.

"Stinger for . . ." Mr. Boone paused dramatically. "Stinger for . . . team 13." Third and final stinger for Kelsey's team!

The audience exploded into applause. Simon let himself look at his parents now. His father had thrown his arms wide to make a *V* for victory. His mother was hugging Jackson's mom.

Simon gave Cody a high five. Jackson

thumped Cody on the back, and then thumped Simon on the back, too. Annika did a happy dance, her braids tossing in time with her feet.

Then, abruptly, she broke off her dance of jubilation. Simon could see in her face that she had remembered that victory for her team meant defeat for her two best friends. Annika darted over to Kelsey and Izzy and gathered them both into a huge hug.

Simon was glad to see them hug her back. In the end, no spelling bee rivalry could ever stop those three from being friends. And Kelsey deserved credit for leading her team to its neck-and-neck second-place finish.

Mr. Boone dismissed the assembly and reminded the winning team—not that they needed any reminder!—to come to the conference room next to his office to eat their prize honey pie at the victors' pie buffet. Their families were invited, too.

Simon turned to Jackson.

"Simon says . . ." he began, hesitantly.

Simon says what?

I'm sorry I act like Super Simon sometimes?

I'm glad you're my friend?

But Jackson cut him off.

"*Jackson* says, Let's go stuff our pie holes with some pie!"

At the pie buffet for the winning teams there were ten different kinds of pie, each one labeled. Some were pies Simon had tasted before: apple, blueberry, cherry, pumpkin, banana cream. Others were unfamiliar: gooseberry, black bottom, Boston cream, shoofly. The honey pie stood on a pedestal in the center of the table.

"Let's each take a sliver of a couple of different ones," Simon's mother said to Jackson's mother, after both moms had swept their sons into an embrace. "Then we can share tastes."

"Let's each take a *whole* slice of *all* of them!" Jackson countered.

"Now, Jackson," his mother warned.

Simon's father grinned at Jackson. To Jackson's mom, he said, "I'd say they've earned their pie. They had some tough words thrown at them, and they didn't flinch."

Well, they had definitely flinched a couple of times.

"Simon knew just about every word," Jackson said. He had already grabbed a big piece of banana cream pie and taken a huge bite. He wiped some whipped cream from his mouth with the side of his hand.

"But Cody was the one who knew *trough*," Simon admitted.

Cody was the one who had spelled the winning word for the entire third-grade bee.

Cody heard his name and flashed them a smile.

Simon helped himself to a slice of honey pie

and took a first taste of its sweet, golden-brown custard filling. Mr. Boone was indeed the best, funniest pie-baking principal there could be.

Would the moment be even sweeter if Simon had won the bee all by himself?

Maybe he wouldn't have won. He wouldn't have messed up on *responsible* if he had been spelling all by himself, but he would have messed up on *trough* instead.

He wouldn't have had a SPECTACULAR SPELLERS T-shirt. He wouldn't have helped teach Annika's dog to spell. He wouldn't have heard Jackson and Cody snoring out spelling words, which, now that he thought about it, had been pretty hilarious.

He wouldn't have been on the same team as his best friend.

Simon went up to Annika, who was getting her second piece of pie.

"Thanks for letting Prime be our mascot," he told her.

"He can spell s-h-a-k-e now," she said. "Kelsey and I taught him this week."

Flushed with the sweetness of victory, Simon found himself wishing Kelsey could be there eating honey pie with them. Maybe she could come over to his house sometime, and they could look up more long, cool words together. Or talk about books they'd both read. They could have fun arguing about which book was the best book in the whole world.

In some ways, Simon actually had more in common with Kelsey than he did with Jackson. Maybe these days Jackson had more in common with Cody than he did with Simon.

But Simon still wanted to play Galaxy Warriors and Amphibian Apocalypse with Jackson sometimes. They could kick a soccer ball around, or shoot baskets, too. Or even play Bird War.

Simon turned back to Jackson.

"Do you think we'll ever play Bird War again?" he asked.

"That dumb game?" Jackson scoffed. Then he said, "Sure!"

Both boys took another bite of Mr. Boone's famous honey pie.

Mr. Boone's Famous Honey Pie Recipe

INGREDIENTS

1 store-bought piecrust
(Mr. Boone makes his own, but he would need to show you exactly how to blend the dough just right with your fingertips, so he said it's fine to use a purchased crust.)

½ cup butter, melted

¼ cup sugar

¼ teaspoon salt

2 tablespoons white cornmeal

¾ cup honey

1 teaspoon vanilla

2 teaspoons white vinegar

3 eggs, lightly beaten

1 cup cream

a sprinkle of coarse salt

DIRECTIONS

Preheat oven to 350 degrees.

With an electric mixer or by hand, combine melted butter, sugar, salt, and cornmeal to make a thick paste. Add honey, vanilla, and vinegar and mix together. Fold in eggs. Add cream and blend. Pour the filling into the piecrust and bake for 45 to 55 minutes, until the filling puffs up and the center is slightly wobbly. Then sprinkle with coarse salt. Let the pie set for a while. Serve either warm or at room temperature.

CLAUDIA MILLS

© Larry Harwood

What did you want to be when you grew up?
I always wanted to be a writer. The only other thing I even considered being was president of the United States. In third grade, I made a hundred-dollar bet with Jimmy Burnett that I would be president someday, but now I'm starting to think maybe Jimmy Burnett is going to win that bet.

When did you realize you wanted to be a writer?
When I was six and my sister was five, my mother gave each of us one of those marble composition notebooks. She told me that my notebook was supposed to be my poetry book, and she told my sister that her notebook was supposed to be her journal. So I started writing poetry, and my sister started keeping a journal, and we both found out that we loved doing it.

What's your most embarrassing childhood memory?

Oh, there are so many! One day in third grade, I decided to run away from school, and I made a very public announcement to that effect. But when I got to the edge of the playground, I realized I had no place to go, so I had to come slinking back again. That memory still makes me cringe.

What's your favorite childhood memory?

We vacationed every summer at a little lake in New Hampshire, and I remember sitting out on the lake in a rowboat, writing poems and drawing pictures and making up stories about imaginary princesses with my sister. Those were very happy days.

As a young person, who did you look up to most?

I mostly looked up to characters in books who were braver and stronger than I was, like Sara Crewe in *A Little Princess,* who loses her beloved father and has to live in poverty in Miss Minchin's cold, miserable garret, but never stops acting like the princess that she feels she is inside. I also looked up to Anne of Green Gables for her spunk in breaking that slate over Gilbert Blythe's head.

What was your favorite thing about school?

It's sort of weird and nerdy to say this, but I loved almost everything about school, and during summer vacations, I'd even cross off the days until school started again. Best of all, I loved any writing assignments and being in plays. In fifth grade, I played the role of stuck-up cousin Annabelle in our classroom play of *Caddie Woodlawn*, and that was wonderful.

What was your least favorite thing about school?
Definitely PE! I was always terrible at PE. I just couldn't do any of the sports, and one time the fourth-grade teacher made the whole class stop and look over at how terribly I was doing this one exercise. I still hate her for that.

What was your first job, and what was your "worst" job?
My first job was working in the junior clothes department at Sears. Back then, three girls worked in one department: one to work the cash register, one to oversee the dressing room, and one to tidy up the clothes racks. I loved tidying up the clothes racks, buttoning up the dresses that needed buttoning. I loved buttoning one dress so much that I bought it, and then found that once I had it at home I had no desire to button it at all anymore. My worst job was being a waitress. I would have done all right if I could have handled just one table at a time, from drinks to salad to main course and then dessert, but my brain could not handle juggling all those different tables at once.

How did you celebrate publishing your first book?
I don't remember celebrating it. Now that I look back, I wish I had. It's a very special moment.

Where do you write your books?

I write all my books in longhand, lying on the couch, using the same clipboard-without-a-clip that I've had for thirty years, always using a white narrow-ruled pad with no margins, and always using a Pilot Razor Point fine-tipped black marker pen.

Is Franklin based on a real school? What about the teachers like Mr. Boone?

No, Franklin is not inspired by any particular real school. Whenever I visit schools (and I love to visit schools), I do scout for material for books, and I definitely have been paying attention to schoolwide reading challenges and how they are organized. While I have never met a principal quite like Mr. Boone, I have come across plenty of principals who are willing to shave their beards or kiss a pig to encourage their students to read.

What makes you laugh out loud?

I always laugh out loud if somebody is trying to do something in an oh-so-serious way and then something goes hideously and publicly awry. That kind of thing makes me howl.

If you could travel in time, where would you go and what would you do?

I'd go back to Amherst, Massachusetts, in the 1850s, and walk by Emily Dickinson's house, and see if she would lower a little basket out the window to me with a fresh-baked muffin and a freshly written poem in it.

What's the best advice you have ever received about writing?

Brenda Ueland says, in *If You Want to Write*, that writing is supposed to be fun, and that if we allow ourselves to let it be fun, stories and poems will just keep pouring out of us. I think she's right.

Do you ever get writer's block? What do you do to get back on track?

I don't, really. My secret is to write for a short, fixed time—usually an hour—every single day. That way I never get burned out from writing, and I never get far enough away from my story that I lose my momentum.

What do you want readers to remember about your books?

I always try to have my main character learn a small but important truth about how to make his or her life better. I know when I think back to favorite books I read a long time ago, it tends to be some little, trivial-but-fun detail that sticks in my head.

GOFISH

ROB SHEPPERSON

What did you want to be when you grew up?
A children's book illustrator. A grown-up one.

When did you realize you wanted to be an illustrator?
Since my father was a minister, I spent every Sunday morning drawing on the church bulletin. The text was limiting ("Hymn #36," "Silent Prayer," "Benediction"), but it introduced the concept of words and pictures working together.

What's your most embarrassing childhood memory?
Being sick in math class. Seems a reasonable response.

What's your favorite childhood memory?
Missing the school bus so that I could walk.

As a young person, who did you look up to most?
My older brother, whose drawings I copied in church. He's still taller.

What was your first job, and what was your "worst" job?
My very, very, very first job was raking pine straw. It's the sort of job you have to quit eventually, 'cause it never ends. My first illustration job was for the local newspaper, *The Ruston Daily Leader*.

How did you celebrate publishing your first book?
My first book was *The Sandman*, and my wife and friends threw a party, but it didn't go all night.

Where do you work on your illustrations?
In a spare bedroom. It has a window, which is useful.

What makes you laugh out loud?
Really bad jokes.

Who is your favorite fictional character?
I wanted to be Stuart Little, but his tiny girlfriend creeped me out.

If you were stranded on a desert island, who would you want for company?
Amelia Earhart. Wouldn't that be a happy ending?

What's the best advice you have ever received about illustrating?
"Make it better." —Steve Heller at the *New York Times Book Review*

What do you want readers to remember about your books?
That they believed in the story.

What would you do if you ever stopped illustrating?
Rest in peace. Hopefully.

Do you have any strange or funny habits? Did you when you were a kid?
As a kid, I played the cornet in the marching band. Seemed normal at the time.

What do you consider to be your greatest accomplishment?
Collaborating with Carolyn Coman on *The Memory Bank*.

If you could travel anywhere in the world, where would you go and what would you do?
Anywhere and everywhere. This is a great planet.

Who is your favorite artist?
Breugel is a favorite for showing how people lived in the sixteenth century, not that I'm that old.

Cody Harmon doesn't love reading, math, spelling,
or really any of the subjects that Mrs. Molina teaches in
her third-grade class. But he lives on a farm and he loves
animals—he even has nine pets—so when the school
holds a pet-show fund-raiser, is it his time to shine?

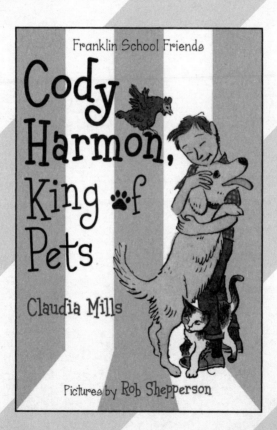

Franklin School Friends

Cody Harmon, King of Pets

Claudia Mills

Pictures by Rob Shepperson

Keep reading for a sneak peek of the fifth book in
the Franklin School Friends series.

1

As Cody Harmon lay on the family room couch after dinner on Sunday evening, his calico cat, Puffball, purred on his chest. His tabby cat, Furface, kneaded his stomach. Rex the golden retriever snored at his feet. And Angus the terrier had just upended the wastepaper basket and was shredding wadded-up tissues all over the family room carpet.

"Angus, no!" Cody hollered.

The cats leaped at the sound. The sheaf of papers on which Cody had been making pig doodles, when he was supposed to be writing a three-page animal report for his teacher, Mrs. Molina, scattered onto the floor.

"Oh, Angus, look what you did!"

Shoving the dog out of the way, Cody started scooping up tissue bits, crumpled wrappers, and the small stuffed giraffe Angus had already destroyed that afternoon. But Cody wasn't mad. He would rather clean up dog mess—even dog poop—than write an animal report any day.

Cody loved animals, all animals.

He did not love writing reports about animals. Especially a report assigned three weeks ago that he had barely begun. Especially a report that was due tomorrow.

His mother came into the room, a baby on each hip: Cody's twin sisters, nine months old and starting to crawl all over the house. Tibbie and Libbie were almost like two more pets, in addition to the dogs, cats, bantam rooster, chickens, and enormous pig out in the pigsty.

"What did he do now?" Cody's mom demanded.

"Nothing," Cody said quickly. "Just got into the trash, but I cleaned it up already."

"That dog is nothing but trouble!" Her eyes fell on the papers still littering the floor, which Angus was now sniffing. "I thought you didn't have any homework this weekend."

"It's not really *homework*. It's an animal report."

"Well, good for you for starting it nice and early." She paused. "When is it due?"

Cody knew better than to lie. "Well, Monday, but—"

"Tomorrow?"

What could Cody say but "I forgot"?

And he *had* forgotten. He'd been busy the whole weekend. A soccer game with his best friend, Tobit Johnson. Helping his mother with the babies. Helping his dad plant the corn. Riding in his dad's pickup to town to spend his twenty dollars of birthday money on tease toys for the cats, squeaker balls for the dogs, and hoof conditioner for Mr. Piggins. How was he supposed to write a pig report, too?

His dad poked his head into the family room doorway. "Everything okay?" he asked with a slow smile.

"Cody has a report due tomorrow," his mom said. "And he hasn't even started it. Have you?" She turned to Cody. "Don't bother answering. I know you haven't."

Well, he had *started* it. Mrs. Molina had made them pick their animal, so he had picked pigs. And she had made them get library books and write a list of the kind of facts they were supposed to find: size, diet, life span, habitat. His books and list were still in his desk at school, buried under all the other work he hadn't remembered to bring home.

"Well, it's only six-thirty now," his dad said mildly. "Bedtime's not for another hour and a half. Let's clear out this menagerie and give the boy a chance to get this thing done."

"Can the animals stay?" Cody asked. "It's a report *on* animals."

His mom harrumphed, but his dad said, "Sure. Just do your best," and gave him another smile.

His dad's encouragement made Cody almost wish he had been working on his report harder.

Back on the couch, with the cats in place and Angus whining to have the squeaker ball tossed for him, Cody looked at Mrs. Molina's assignment sheet. Awake now, Rex nuzzled Cody's knee, as if worried that his boy had such a big report to write so quickly.

"You must get your animal facts from at least two different sources. These must be books or magazines, not the Internet," read the instructions.

Cody doubted everyone in his class would do that. Perfect Simon Ellis would have ten—or twenty, or a hundred—sources, but no one else in

the Franklin School third grade was like Simon.
Well, Kelsey Green would have a lot of sources,
too. Kelsey loved to read. But Tobit probably
only had one.

Zero wasn't that much less than one.

Besides, if there was one thing Cody knew
about, it was pigs. He could be his own source.

He picked up his pencil and started writing.

I like pigs. Pigs are smart. People think
pigs are dirty, but pigs are clean. I
like pigs a LOT.

That was a good start.

Pigs eat slops from a trough. My pig is
called Mr. Piggins.

Six whole sentences! That was long enough
for one page, and he could add another page

with a picture. Cody set his completed page on the floor and, on a second sheet of paper, started to draw a portrait of Mr. Piggins from memory.

It wasn't like he'd get a good grade anyway. Mrs. Molina never gave him good grades on anything. He had the worst grades in the class, even worse than Tobit's.

But no one else had as many pets as he did.

Cody looked over at Angus, who had pieces of something white and crumpled hanging out of his mouth. Pieces of Cody's pig report.

"Angus, no!"

It was too late.

Now he had to write the whole dumb report all over again.

Don't miss any of the
Franklin School Friends
books!